CHARLIE MALARKEY
AND THE SINGING MOOSE

By

William Kennedy

and

Brendan Kennedy

Illustrated by

S. D. Schindler

Viking

The authors dedicate this book
to those who made it possible:
Each other,
the mooses of North America,
and
Frank Sinatra.

VIKING
Published by the Penguin Group
Penguin Books USA Inc., 375 Hudson Street, New York, New York 10014, U.S.A.
Penguin Books Ltd, 27 Wrights Lane, London W8 5TZ, England
Penguin Books Australia Ltd, Ringwood, Victoria, Australia
Penguin Books Canada Ltd, 10 Alcorn Avenue, Toronto, Ontario, Canada M4V 3B2
Penguin Books (N.Z.) Ltd, 182–190 Wairau Road, Auckland 10, New Zealand

Penguin Books Ltd, Registered Offices: Harmondsworth, Middlesex, England

First published in 1994 by Viking, a division of Penguin Books USA Inc.

1   3   5   7   9   10   8   6   4   2

Text copyright © William Kennedy and Brendan Kennedy, 1994
Illustrations copyright © S. D. Schindler, 1994   All rights reserved
Title design by Maria Demopoulos

Library of Congress Cataloging-in-Publication Data
Kennedy, William
Charlie Malarkey and the singing moose / by William Kennedy and
Brendan Kennedy; illustrated by S. D. Schindler.   p.   cm.
Summary: Charlie Malarkey and his friend Iggy rescue Barnaby,
a singing moose with a magic necktie, from the clutches of his dastardly trainer.
ISBN 0-670-84605-8
[1. Moose—Fiction.   2. Neckties—Fiction.]
I. Kennedy, Brendan.   II. Schindler, S. D., ill.   III. Title.
PZ7.K3867Ck 1994 [Fic]—dc20   93-41483 CIP AC

Printed in Singapore   Set in ITC Zapf International

O nce upon a time Charlie Malarkey and his friend
Iggy Gowalowicz were on their way to the circus.

"Acrobats," said Iggy.

"Acrobats?" said Charlie.

"Acrobats are my favorite," said Iggy.

"Acrobats are boring," said Charlie. "I want to see Barnaby the moose."

"Barnaby the moose? What does he do?"

"He sings songs."

"Moose songs?" asked Iggy.

"Moose songs, all kinds of songs," said Charlie. "At least that's what the posters say." Then he and Iggy bought tickets and entered the circus tent.

After the parade of lions, tigers, elephants, and clowns was over, the lights went down and the ringmaster spoke to the audience.

"Ladies and gentlemen," he said, "now, for the very first time anywhere in the world, Ralph T. Bungaroo, the world's greatest moose trainer, presents his singing moose, Barnaby!"

Suddenly the lights went out and a spotlight shone on a short fat man in a white suit, black boots, and a jungle helmet. He was standing beside a very large moose who was chained to a wagon. The moose was at least ten feet tall, his antlers were six feet wide, and he was wearing a long black-and-white polka-dot necktie. Charlie couldn't help noticing he looked very sad.

"Are you ready, Barnaby?"
Ralph T. Bungaroo asked the moose.

The moose looked at his keeper and nodded
what looked to Charlie like a very sad nod. Then
Barnaby raised his head, opened his enormous
mouth, and sang "Fly Me to the Moose."

The crowd screamed with pleasure and, as Barnaby
continued to sing, many women in the audience swooned,
for this was obviously a very romantic moose.

He sang "Moose Indigo," "Here's to You, Mooses Robinson," and ended
with "A Moose Over Troubled Water." The crowd stomped and cheered and
threw hats in the air, but Barnaby did not smile. He just lowered his head as
Ralph T. Bungaroo led him back into his cage.

"Wow," Iggy said, "I didn't know mooses could sing."

"Most can't," said Charlie.

After the circus was over Charlie and Iggy went back to see the animals. As they got closer to Barnaby's cage Charlie picked up something from the ground.

"Hey look, Ig," he said, "it's Barnaby's necktie."

"That's the biggest necktie I ever saw," Iggy said.

"An ordinary tie wouldn't fit Barnaby," said Charlie.

They walked to Barnaby's cage and found him still looking sad.

"Um . . . Mister Barnaby?" Charlie said.

"Don't call me mister," Barnaby said. "I'm only a moose."

"My friend Iggy and I wanted to tell you we really liked your singing."

Barnaby just nodded and looked away.

"We also found your tie," Charlie added.

Barnaby looked up, very excited.

"My tie? You found my tie? That's terrific!" And he did a little moose dance. "Don't let Bungaroo get it. That tie is magic. It helps you sing."

"You can't sing without it?" said Charlie.

"I can, but then I sound like any other moose."

"How do you know all the words?" Iggy asked.

"The tie knows the words," said Barnaby.

Just then Ralph T. Bungaroo came around the corner and yelled, "Hey, what are you two kids doing to my moose?"

Iggy stepped in front of Charlie to hide the necktie and said, "We were just telling him what a great singer he is."

"He already knows that," said Bungaroo. "Now get lost."

So Charlie and Iggy pretended to leave, but hid behind the tattooed lady's wagon. When Bungaroo went off muttering, "I gotta find that necktie," the boys sneaked back to Barnaby.

"Pssst . . . Mister Barnaby?" said Charlie. "What do you want me to do with this necktie?"

"Guard it with your life. And don't call me mister. I'm only a moose."

So Charlie put the tie under his jacket and he and Iggy left the circus.

At home Charlie hid the necktie in his toy chest and then his mother made him and Max, his pet monkey, their favorite dinner—peanut butter sandwiches with duck sauce.

"Did you enjoy the circus, Charlie?" Mrs. Malarkey asked.

"It was great," Charlie said. "We saw the singing moose."

"Moose don't sing, Charlie. Somebody probably sang for him."

Charlie rolled his eyes and decided not to argue. Max ate his sandwich in one big bite, then he and Charlie went to their room, where they heard a strange sound coming from the toy chest.

Charlie opened the chest and there was his rubber kangaroo singing "Waltzing Matilda." Charlie reached into the chest and picked up the necktie and the kangaroo stopped singing. He touched the tie to his toy policeman, who immediately started to sing "Jailhouse Rock."

"This is fantastic," Charlie said to Max, who leaped on top of a lamp and hung by his tail, watching. Charlie put his stuffed ostrich on top of the tie, and the ostrich started to sing "I've Got My Head in the Sand Over You."

The slow, dreamy music made Charlie sleepy, so he put Max in his cage and hid the necktie under his pillow. As he closed his eyes he heard his pillow humming "Rock-a-Bye Baby," which he hadn't heard since he was a very small boy. And he went right to sleep.

The next morning Max woke up before Charlie, climbed down from his cage, and saw the necktie sticking out from under Charlie's pillow. Max pulled it free, climbed out the window onto a tree branch, and scrambled down onto the front porch. He sat on the tie and started to whistle. The mailman arrived just then and couldn't believe his eyes and ears.

"You're whistling," the mailman said. "Can you sing too?"

"I've got a lovely bunch of coconuts," Max sang.

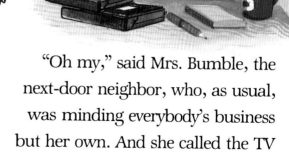

"Oh my," said Mrs. Bumble, the next-door neighbor, who, as usual, was minding everybody's business but her own. And she called the TV station to report what she saw at the Malarkeys'.

Across town Bungaroo was in his wagon, yelling at his assistant, Mortimer Mopp, a tall, thin, stringbean fellow whose hair hung down over his face. Mortimer was watching TV and waiting for his favorite show, "Bingo-Bongo Baseball."

"If we don't find that necktie soon," said Bungaroo, "I'm ruined. That moose can't sing a note without the tie, and the circus owner won't pay me if the moose doesn't sing."

"Hey, Ralph," said Mortimer Mopp, "there's a monkey on TV with a necktie like Barnaby's."

"What are you babbling about?" snapped Bungaroo, and he went to the TV.

"It's incredible," said the TV announcer. "We're here in North Albany watching a monkey swinging from a necktie on a front porch, and he's singing 'I'm a Monkey Doodle Dandy.'"

Mrs. Bumble came over to the announcer and said, "That monkey has a marvelous voice. I've known him ever since Charlie Malarkey brought him home, but I never knew he could carry a tune."

Bungaroo slapped Mopp on the head. "You goofy bump," he said. "That *is* Barnaby's necktie. Let's go get it."

Charlie woke up to the noise
of a crowd cheering outside his bedroom window.
He dressed and ran down to the porch, where Max was singing for
the TV camera. Charlie picked up Max and the tie, much to the disappoint-
ment of the crowd, and said, "Time for Max to have breakfast, folks."

Mrs. Malarkey was in the kitchen, mixing broccoli-and-banana juice for
Max, when Charlie came in. "Charlie, who are all those people on the front
lawn?" she asked.

"They were watching Max sing," Charlie explained.

"Indeed," said Mrs. Malarkey. "A singing moose and now a singing
monkey. Next you'll be telling me your toys can sing too." And Charlie, rather
than contradict his mother, only rolled his eyes again. She went to the parlor
to make a telephone call.

Just then the doorbell rang. It was Iggy.

"I saw Max on TV so I came over," Iggy said. "I didn't know monkeys could sing like that."

"Most can't," said Charlie. "Max swiped Barnaby's tie from under my pillow this morning."

"You better hide it or he'll steal it again," Iggy said. "Put it in the stove."

"No, my mother might cook it," Charlie said.

"How about the freezer? Nobody puts neckties in the freezer these days."

"Great idea, Ig," Charlie said, and he opened the freezer and buried the tie under a large box of fish sticks.

"Charlie," said Mrs. Malarkey, hanging up the telephone and coming into the kitchen, "I'm going to the circus with Mrs. Bumble. When I get back I don't want to hear any more stories about singing animals." She plopped on her best hat, the one with the drooping flower, and out she went.

A few minutes later the door flew open and in stormed Ralph T. Bungaroo, with Mortimer Mopp right behind him.

"Okay, Malarkey," growled Bungaroo, "I've had enough of you and your pal. Hand over that tie, or Mortimer will turn your monkey into meatballs."

"I make great meatballs," said Mortimer with a nasty chuckle, and he grabbed Max and popped him into a cloth bag.

"I don't have the tie," said Charlie. "I swapped it."

"What do you mean, you swapped it?" yelled Bungaroo.

"I traded it for a five-year supply of ice cream."

"Baloney sauce," Bungaroo snarled. "I'll bet it's here somewhere," and he and Mopp looked behind the piano, in the cookie jar, in the toy chest, under Charlie's pillow. When Mopp opened the freezer door, Charlie distracted him by spilling Max's broccoli-and-banana juice on his tennis shoes. And a good thing it was, because the four fish on the fish-sticks box were singing "By the Sea" in barbershop harmony.

Bungaroo grew very angry and shook his cigar at Charlie. "Listen, Malarkey, if that necktie isn't in my wagon in one hour, your monkey is hot-dog meat."

Then he and Mopp, who had Max in the bag, stomped out.

"Gosh, Charlie," said Iggy,
"why did you say you swapped the tie?"

"If we don't do something to stop Bungaroo," Charlie said,
"Barnaby will be a prisoner in the circus for his whole life."

"What about Max? You think they'd really hurt him?"

"You never can tell with nasty guys," Charlie said.

"Maybe we should go to the cops," said Iggy.

"No," said Charlie. "I have a plan. . . ."

He took the tie out of the freezer, tucked it under his shirt, and put
on his baseball jacket. Then he and Iggy headed for the circus.

Hundreds of people were lined up to buy circus tickets. Everybody was asking the same question: "Does the moose sing today?"

Charlie and Iggy found Bungaroo's wagon, peeked in, and saw Bungaroo pacing up and down while Mortimer Mopp watched "Bingo-Bongo Baseball." They saw Max, chained to the wall, looking very unhappy. "If that Malarkey kid doesn't bring my tie back I'll hang him, and his monkey, by their little toes," said Bungaroo. "This circus is only the beginning. The whole world will pay to hear Barnaby sing"—he laughed an evil laugh—"and I'll be rich."

"Me too, Ralph?" asked Mortimer Mopp.

"We'll see," said Bungaroo.

Charlie and Iggy went to Barnaby's cage. "Pssst . . . it's us," Charlie whispered. "The guys who found your tie."

Barnaby raised his head. "My tie. Is it safe?"

"It's under my shirt," said Charlie. "Bungaroo kidnapped my monkey, and he says he'll hurt him if I don't give him the tie."

"I'll take care of Bungaroo," Barnaby said. "Just give me that tie and get me out of this cage."

Charlie pulled the tie from under his shirt and slipped it through the bars. Barnaby sat on the tie and softly sang "Moosie in the Sky with Diamonds."

"If you sing loud," Charlie said, "Bungaroo will come out to see you, and then we can go in and get his keys."

"You know, Charlie," Barnaby said, "you're the smartest person I ever met who wasn't a moose."

So Charlie and Iggy hid behind the wagon owned by Henry, the Human Cannonball, and then they heard Barnaby singing, at the top of his voice, "Sergeant Pepper's Lonely Moose Club Band."

Inside the wagon Bungaroo stood up from his chair so fast he slipped on the rug and fell into his cactus plant. "The moose is singing!" he screamed.

"That's a moose?" Mopp said. "It sounded like Frank Sinatra."

Bungaroo hit Mopp on the top of the head. "You bumpy goof! Get out there and see what's going on." And Mopp tumbled out of the wagon, with Bungaroo right behind him.

Charlie and Iggy tiptoed into the wagon, found the keys, and unlocked Max's chain. Max jumped onto Charlie's shoulder, then they went outside and hid behind the wagon of Big Buster, the Strongest Man in the World.

The circus owner came running up to Bungaroo. "I thought I heard the moose singing," he said.

"Me too," said Bungaroo. He asked Barnaby, "Were you just singing?"

Barnaby, looking sad and sitting on his necktie (if you looked closely you could see the edge of it), said only, "Moop."

"Moop?" said the owner. "What does he mean, moop? Moose don't say moop. Is he going to sing?"

"Moop," said Barnaby.

"Listen, Bungaroo," the owner said, "I don't pay you for moop. People want their money back. Is he singing or isn't he?"

"He'll sing," Bungaroo said. "He's just getting a sore throat."

"If he don't sing," the owner said, "you're in big trouble." And he went back to the big tent to calm down the customers.

When Bungaroo left, Charlie opened Barnaby's cage and unlocked his leg chain. Barnaby leaped out.

"This moose is loose!" he roared. He lowered his head to let Charlie put on his necktie, and then Iggy and Charlie climbed onto his back. Barnaby trotted toward the ticket booth singing "There's No Business Like Moose Business," louder than Charlie had ever heard him sing.

"It's the singing moose!" somebody yelled, and cheers rose up from the crowd at the ticket booth as Barnaby trotted into the tent, still singing. People forgot about getting their money back and rushed in to take their seats. Inside, Barnaby galloped around the center ring.

Charlie, Iggy, and Max had never been so happy. They waved to everybody. Charlie's mother waved back, but she couldn't believe what she was seeing. She turned to Mrs. Bumble and said, "My son riding on a singing moose! What will Charlie think of next?"

Then Bungaroo entered the center ring and spoke into the microphone. "Allow me to introduce myself, ladies and gentlemen. I am Ralph T. Bungaroo, the world's greatest moose trainer, who today is bringing you Barnaby, the singing moose!"

When Barnaby heard this, he stopped singing, ran over to Bungaroo, and, with his antlers, tossed him high into the air.

"The moose has gone wild," screamed a woman in the audience.

"Somebody call the police!" a man yelled.

When Barnaby again tossed Bungaroo into the air the microphone went flying and Charlie caught it. "Ralph T. Bungaroo isn't a moose trainer," Charlie said to the crowd, "he's a moose-napper. He kept Barnaby in chains and made him sing for money. Today Barnaby is singing as a free moose."

"Boooooo, boooooo, Bungaroo," the crowd hooted, "booooo, boooooo, Bungaroo."

And people hissed and shook their fists at the villain, who was now dangling sideways from Barnaby's antlers.

One clown hit Bungaroo with a pie, and another poured water on his head from a sprinkling can. The crowd laughed and cheered, and then Big Buster, the Strongest Man in the World, came over and with one hand lifted up Bungaroo and shoved him feet-first into the barrel of Henry the Human Cannonball's big cannon. Henry lit the fuse, the cannon boomed, and Bungaroo flew toward the far end of the tent.

"Bye-bye, Bungaroo," the crowd chanted, "bye-bye, Bungaroo."

When Bungaroo landed in the safety net, two policemen collared him and arrested him for moose-napping in the first degree. Mortimer Mopp ran off when he saw Bungaroo in the cannon, and when last seen was selling bottled broccoli-and-banana juice in the Fiji Islands.

In the final circus parade Charlie and Iggy rode on Barnaby's back. Max, swinging from Barnaby's necktie, sang two choruses of "Yes, We Have No Bananas" with Barnaby.

"Look how well my Charlie rides that moose," Mrs. Malarkey said to Mrs. Bumble. "Why, I'll bet he could be president someday."

The parade ended, the tent exploded with applause, and everyone said it was the best show they'd ever seen.

Afterward, Mrs. Malarkey made a big bowl of Barnaby's favorite dessert, chocolate mousse, and served it on her front porch. Barnaby ate three helpings, and thanked the Malarkeys and Iggy for everything. Now, he said, he was going back to being an ordinary moose who only sang in the shower.

"You could never be just an ordinary moose," Charlie said to him, patting him on the neck. "You'll bring music wherever you go in the world."

"Not if you and Iggy hadn't saved me," Barnaby said.

Barnaby then asked Mrs. Malarkey to cut a small piece off his necktie and pin it to Max's jacket. When she did this Max burst into a fast eight bars of "Monkeys on Parade," and Barnaby said Max had a great future in music.

Barnaby said good-bye to the Malarkeys and Iggy, then trotted down the street, waving his antlers to all the neighborhood people who had turned out to see him off.

As he went he sang one more song for them:

Meet me tonight in mooseland,
Under the silvery moon.
Meet me tonight in mooseland,
There we will sing our tune.
Come with the moose tones rising,
In your dear voice, please do.
Meet me in mooseland,
Sweet moosey mooseland,
That's where our dreams come true.

The neighbors on the street all cheered and waved good-bye, and as Barnaby was going around the corner Charlie spoke for everybody's feelings when he said, "There goes one great moose."